THE RIVER TROLL
SPECIAL COLOR EDITION

Durvile & UpRoute Books

UPROUTE IMPRINT OF DURVILE PUBLICATIONS LTD.

Calgary, Alberta, Canada
durvile.com

Copyright © 2021 Rich Théroux

LIBRARY AND ARCHIVES CATALOGUING IN PUBLICATIONS DATA

The River Troll: A Story about Love in Color
Théroux, Rich, author

1. Young Adult Fiction
2. Canadian Poetry | 3. Canadian Art | 4. Magic Realism

Every River Lit Series. Series editor, Lorene Shyba

978-1-9888249-4-9 (pbk)
978-1-988824-78-9 (ebook)
978-1-988824-79-6 (audiobook)

Cover paintings and paintings throughout the book: Rich Théroux.
Poems in the book except "In Color" previously published in
A Wake in the Undertow, Durvile Publications, 2017.

Durvile Publications recognizes the traditional land upon which our studios rest.
The Indigenous Peoples of Southern Alberta include the
Siksika, Piikani, and Kainai of the Blackfoot Confederacy; the Dene Tsuut'ina;
and the Chiniki, Bearspaw, and Wesley Stoney Nakoda First Nations;
and the Region 3 Métis Nation of Alberta.

Durvile Publications would like to acknowledge the financial support of
the Government of Canada through Canadian Heritage Canada Book Fund
and the Government of Alberta, Alberta Media Fund.

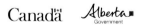

Printed in Canada. Second edition, second printing. 2022.
First edition ISBN is 978-1-988824-77-2

RICH THÉROUX

THE RIVER TROLL

a story
about love
in color

DURVILE &
UpRoute Books

Calgary, Alberta, Canada

Thanks to

Alexander Eliot

Lorene Shyba

Jessica Theroux

Theresa, Mitchell, Robin, Oliver, and Felix

For the dandelions,

the magpies, and

the people who love them.

Also by Rich Théroux

Stop Making Art and Die
    A Survival Guide for Artists

A Wake in the Undertow
    Rumble House Poems
    With Jess Szabo

Rumblesat Art From the Edge of Space
    With Jim Parker & Lorene Shyba

One

IN COLOR

This is a poem
about color

We made my book once in black
and white

And it felt fine
but some of the magic was
hidden

I had a chance to reprint
in color

And I leapt on it

It felt
so
great

There are secrets about color in this book
One, the one you might think the least true

Is the most true

Be careful in school
Your teachers will get very upset
if you tell them you can mix
Red
Yellow
Or
Blue

(Be) Fore Word AFTERWORD

If you haven't read this book, maybe you should wait and read this later. I had a chance to bring the color back into the art work. It's been about two years since I wrote The River Troll and seven months (now) since the first edition. Between then and now, I've grown a little and I've come to understand we left our hero on an awkward ledge. We don't know if he's ready or not ready to dive in headlong.

I find I read it now with two potentially different endings. As a writer I can still grow and see new things, but our narrator, at the risk of changing the ending, has been suspended in time, like a moth preserved flat in the pages of a book.

I wonder if he'll ever pull his head out of his ass, ready to truly accept the love waiting for him.

With love,
Rich Théroux

NEXT TO ME IS JESS, the most beautiful woman I have ever seen. Naked. Snoring a little. She sleeps with her mouth wide open and her breath will have a tang in the morning.

I can't reach the record player. It used to be next to the bed. But if I get up I'm going on a walk. The bedsheets are sweaty. I should have opened the window, but if I get up to open the window, I'm going on a walk. I have to teach in the morning. I should try and sleep, but it's June, it's really warm and I think I'm just going to go.

For a walk.

I slide out of bed,
pull on my jeans
careful not to catch
my junk in the zipper.
I dip into a cotton t-shirt,
and slide into sneakers
        without socks.

Socks are relevant to this story
because it means if
I stay out too late
        I'll get blisters.

I look for my keys in the dark.
In my head as I lock the front
door, I see a gang of pirates letting
themselves in, kidnapping my
sleeping beauty.

The lock clanks shut.

I take the stairs and I step over
piles of poop on the sixth and
fourth floors. Poop piles in the
stairwell get treated with some
white spray substance.
It's the first half of a clean-up
effort. I wonder what the second
half looks like.

I'm going to take my time, and let
things happen.

There's a drunk in the lobby. He lives about twenty blocks away. He has this hustle where he sits on leg folded underneath him so it looks amputated at the knee. He sits in our lobby or in the alley or at the door of the liquor store across the street and he asks people for help. He takes ambulances instead of taxis, and he's mean.

I have to meet this guy all over again, every time. He's got no memory of yesterday.

He calls out, *Hey Friend* then something unintelligible. I can sort of hear, but I pretend I can't hear and I'm angry at myself because I help this guy out all the time. I tap my tiny headphones, and Duke Ellington and his orchestra light up the night.

Scan for ch.1 animation

TWO

I STEP INTO THE STREET and
the wind licks my shirt, tugs
my sleeve from my ruined arm
and thwaps it back and forth, I
hope, all night long.

The brewery is puffing gobs of
yeast into the warm night air.
I go straight at the corner.
I don't want to go near the
gallery and get sucked inside
and have to clean up.

I'll wander down to the river.
I cross as many bridges as I
can to keep the vampires away.
Streets downtown are bright.

You see half as many stars as you
would in the suburbs, and a hundredth
of what you might see in the country,
but city lights are bright. Sometimes
the lights are programmed to filter
through all the rainbow colors.
I suppose the city lights are every bit
as beautiful as the stars. These are my
stars, the lights on my not-very-busy
downtown streets.

My sleepy metropolis. It gets busy on
8th Avenue but it's empty by 9th. I can
be as social or as antisocial as I like.

It's mostly toothless demons
this time of night.
I head for the river because the
toothless demons don't cross bridges
either. They sit at the edges of the river
popping and pooping and peeing.
The shore is as dirty as the poop-filled
river but the bridges are pristine.

Under the bridge
is a different matter.
Under the bridge is a troll.
He's so ugly
you can't look him in the eye.
You'd need to climb up his chest
to look him in the eye,
but you can't because
his clothes are slimy from a
thousand years of
eating sweaty children.

He won't eat me, I'm too salty.

What good do you do me, he says.
He's not as British as you'd expect.

What good do you do me? I say.
I use my deepest voice to show him
I'm not afraid.

Bah, I should eat you.
        Bug off, you ugly clout.

He smiles,
I think I will eat you tonight.

I spit at him,
near him,
but not on him.
If I hit him he'd kill me,
but I find the closer I get
the harder he laughs.

        Tell me a story you dirty beast.

What story tonight?
    Tell me a story about how true love
is like a butterfly.

And why should I tell you such a story?
    Because I'll tell the children and it
will make them happy and I know you
like the taste of happy children best.
Tell me a butterfly story and I'll tell
the sad children at school and they will
make better meals.

It's a lie,
none of your children ever come my way.

I can't lie to a troll.
I tell them to stay away, it's true,
but imagine how good they would taste
if they choose not to listen.

You're a mean little man (says he).

> Go on.

He sits.
Strangely when he sits under the bridge
his head is still near the roof, wasn't his
head touching the roof when he was
standing?
He sits.
He still fills the space.

*I'll tell you a story, but you better send
a tasty child my way or
I'm not telling you any more.*

It's a story about love. And how to love.
The troll holds out his giant hand.

*This hand is love, See? And you puny
people really have no idea how to love.*

See?

He pushes his palm into my face.

Now this is being loved, and a bird-like moth
flutters into his bloated hand.

You love the butterfly, see?

The moth chews at the algae
in the cracks of his skin.

You love the pretty butterfly.

    That's a moth.

You love the pretty butterfly,
but it's a butter fly, it's not a butter sit.

On cue the moth flies away and the troll sits,
palm open. He explains the butterfly's job is to
fly away, but that we do not understand love.

    That's a shitty story.

Just wait. So we wait.
We wait a very long time and
the moth flies back and the troll says,

So you wait and you keep your hand open
and the butterfly comes back.
But only when it chooses to.

And the moth flies away.

This happens several times
with no explanation,
but the troll is patient and
I've got nothing better to do.
Finally, the moth comes back.
The troll says, *You—*
Your kind doesn't understand love.

He squeezes his fist shut,
veins and sinew gnash.

You hold onto love like this, he says,
opening his hand to the
juicy mess in his palm.
He licks it off, curls his finger back
with his thumb and flicks me a
hundred yards away.

I soar through the warm air, I judge
my trajectory by the faintness
of his laughter.

I land softly in the bosom
of a one-eyed witch giantess.
She plucks me by my pant leg
and lowers me
to the ground.

That was lucky, I say, turning myself
upright.

Nonsense, she says. *There's no such thing as luck.*
There's ready and not ready.

Tell me more, I say to the giantess.

She folds her tit back into her blouse
and says dismissively,
You are not ready.

She takes two gigantic steps
                        and she is gone.

Scan

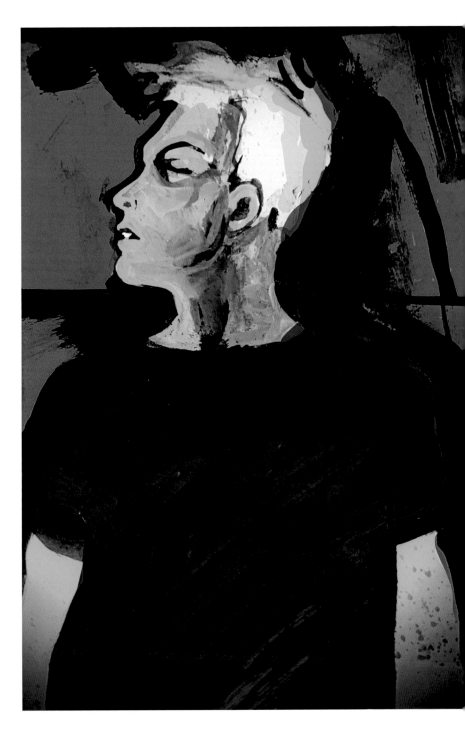

THREE

I'M HUNGRY. That is the trouble with late-night walks. The overeating. Nothing is open, I do not desire gas station food.

I get to the river. Now, do I want to walk towards the source or towards the ocean? Here the river flows away from the ocean. Here the two rivers meet. I choose the source. There's a sweaty man in cowboy boots and no pants sitting on a bench. Those boots must be chafing.

A slim man with no legs at all starts to follow me. Be gone dead man I say and he turns away. I'm not in the mood to walk with the dead. It might be better to leave this magic river. A few hundred steps later I cross some railway tracks. I wet my sneakers on the damp grass and make my way back to pavement.

I walk home, let myself in.
Jess is safe and I climb into bed,
wet cuffs of my jeans, the alarm
rings, she gets out of bed
and makes coffee.

I close my eyes and for three
wonderful minutes I sleep.

. . .

I drive Jess to work.
And then drive
thirty more minutes
on the highway to my school.

Dead things lie on the road and a mountainous
strip of torn paper splits the ground from the sky.
It is beautiful.
I swerve all over hell forgetting to look at the road.
I haven't hit anything which by the look of things
means I'm the only one.
I listen to jazz on the way to work.
Sometimes I listen to recordings of
books about jazz, I like to put them on
double time and read twice as much.

I'm a good listener.

In the springtime, the sunrise is always behind me
and the traffic comes the other way. Real estate
agents should advise their clients to live east of
their work, but I suspect no one ever has. Perhaps
they get more return clients this way. Either way
I'm happy to drive to work, whatever Jess' words
were leaving the car linger on my mind.

Eventually I get to the parking lot.
I let the music die and I think if I could
wear jeans and listen to Charlie Parker all day
I'd probably do this job for free.

As it is I think I'll kill myself in the next few years.

I unload my trunk and I carry in the
things I took out to my trunk last night.
Why do I carry this baggage home if
not for the inevitable pantomime?

Sisyphus.

The minotaur I had coffee with in the
cab of my car runs off.

Bugger off moose head! I yelled,
and he waves.

None of the other teachers see him
vanish into the trees.
That mother bugger could listen to
Charlie Parker all day if he wanted to.

Freeloader.

Dear Sisyphus
How does it look
When you turn over?
What do you mean?
How does it look
When you restart
At the bottom?
I'm sorry?
When you reach the peak
And have to start over?
How does it look to ...
How does what look?
   ... to start over
What?
   ...what are you doing there
I'm pushing this rock
Of course I am
   ... where are you going
To the top
Of course I am
   ... how long until you get there
I don't know
It's been taking a while
Why so long?
I keep having to start over
Oh, and what does that look like?
...
It looks like morning

The school lights hurt my eyes. The kids are extra needy today. Everyone is losing their collective mind. It's the end of the year, the Grade 7s don't know who the heck they are anymore all the way up the chain to the Grade 12s who are splitting bricks over life, and suddenly they realize they know bugger all after twelve long years.

I do my best to get them through the day. I eat lunch in my room so I won't have to speak to the other teachers. The cool ones make their way to the art room, the lost and disenfranchised kids are there too.

One young lady has a broken heart about her friend who doesn't love her the way she needs her to.

I tell her the story of the butterfly, but it doesn't help.

Maybe it does.

How would anyone ever really know?

I keep telling them that is what art is
for. Sometimes they seem to listen.

At the end of the day I am tired.
I meet my minotaur friend at the car
and we drive home to pick up Jess.
Tonight is laundry and a shop at the
grocery store and the ecstasy of it
could kill you if you weren't careful.

Because of the rain and my autism
I get lost on the way.

Eventually I make the right turn and
she is there waiting on the steps of
her school. You might think she is
one of the goddesses in this story.
But she is just as she seems, unlikely,
but as real as wind or sea. You might
be wondering if I've made this all up.

Scan

In the car, a song comes on the radio. It's got no words but I compose my own lyrics no one will ever hear.

> For ages I watched the tigers in their cages
> in I crept in the pitch of night
> while the keepers slept
> and unlocked
> the gates
> some ran
> some stayed
> I hoped some might love me
> I knew some would hate me
> the truly bitter lingered
> and then they ate me.

FOUR

I'T'S A LONG RIDE UP the elevator, but it's the price of a million-dollar view.

In the summer the ants and the roaches never make it up this high and we sit and eat and drink and listen to Satchmo blow his horn all summer long and we won't ever see a mosquito and I like the way the building shakes when the train rumbles by.

If you've ever wondered what happened to dragons. Not so long ago, they decided to bury themselves in armour, they dress like trains and they slither back and forth across the country. At night you can hear them clashing as they have their dragon belly battles over the food goods packed under their armour.

You may not believe in conspiracy, but
you should know all the trains you've
ever seen are really dragons in disguise.
And they are surly.

· · ·

Some cheese and some black forest ham
and a few noodles and jalapeños fall
into a pot and the sun is setting on the
balcony and the neighbours in every
language imaginable are yelling to turn
the music up or turn it down, but it won't
budge as long as I'm alive. The sun turns
red and goes out. We sit and drink and
kiss and wait for time to close our eyes
and for the awake to go away.

A few things happen, and then I'm
brushing my teeth and she's washing off
her face. And the lights go out, all but
the ones that shine up from the road and
dance irrational Mesopotamian dances
on the wall.

Eventually Jess is asleep and I am
thinking I should try a little harder
to fall asleep too.

I was up all last night and the night
before talking to the river troll. Jess is
asleep and I give it one last try.
I take a jar of spicy liniments and I
rub down my battered ankles and my
swollen knee and then I rub my eyes
and let the liniments burn my eyes
shut. Water streams down my cheeks
before the blinding pain subsides. I
pass out afraid I'll wake up blind. I
drop into a deep sleep and I go into
the house with all the shrinking
hallways that get narrower and more
hidden and I squeeze myself into
tinier passages until I find myself in
the most interesting room I have ever
been to in my life.

There I sit with the clever monkey.
The clever monkey gives me hits and
misses about the secrets of life.

Did you win that award you wanted?
    They don't give you awards until you don't
need them. By the time they can even see you,
you're looking down from the clouds and they
are frantically waving up at you for attention.

The clever monkey looks at me for a very long
time. I've got all night.

Listen here, mother hugger, you have to move,
says the clever monkey. It's a miracle
to see his lips wrap around the words.
*You see you ugly mother hugger you just
want to sit and the truth is you have to move.
Yoga is for my ass! You better get up and go for
a run, because the thing that runs this place
pays your rent, so to say. That thing has a plan
for you and it's to move.*

I'm kind of speechless.

You ever watch hockey?
    No.
You've seen it though?
    Yes.
What happens?
    Uh?

*Rubber puck goes here and there then it
goes in the net and people yell at the TV.*
    Yeah—

But it's like, then what?
    Another goal?

And the clever monkey says *exactly.*

    So what does it mean?

*It means mother hugger that you've got
to move. God or whatever you want to
call her wants you to move and if you
don't they get mad.*

Yeah. I say, what kind of wisdom do I expect, if I'm in the secret room of the bendy house then this is a dream and that means any wisdom I get from this dream is from my own head and probably not much good. Luckily I'm good-looking and I can take a punch, so I carry on.

The minotaur is next to me, he says *listen here this is important* and I'm sure he's real, but not sure how he got into my dream.

Clever monkey: *See, when your team wins the hockey you should be happy and when your team loses the hockey you should be sad. It's all a mirage to keep you from a revolution, to give you the sense you've done something. But when your team loses you sulk and go to bed but should they win, like a cup, like a really big win, the whole city gets out and tips over cars and lights garbage bins on fire.*

Right.

They should be happy but they destroy their homes.

Right.

Because they felt like they were on the move,
they feel the rush of the move they feel the joy of
the move but they sit through it. Like a bunch of
ninny butter-sits.

Oh crap, I say, I think I get it and the buzzer
goes and Jess gets up and makes coffee and I lay
there thinking, I could use about three more
minutes of sleep.

We drink the coffee and we get in the car
and she gets out of the car and my friend the
minotaur gets in and I turn off the music.
I sit and he looks at me and he blinks his big fat
brown bulging cow eyes innocently at me and
finally he says, *What?*

I'm like, what was all that last night?

He smiles, *You know I can't speak.*

Scan

I put the key in the car and drive to work,
I don't even look at him.

FIVE

TODAY IS AN EXCEPTIONAL DAY. I get
into work and I open my computer.
It's not charged so I need to find the
plug to put it in the wall and I open my
email and it reads, *something, something,
something, something, report cards—*

Nope, I can't deal with this right now, I
put down the lid and let it charge. This
lady I don't even know what she does,
she's not my boss, but she sticks her head
in my room and asks me, *Is it ready to
print yet?* and I'm silent, she turns red
and a greyhound comes out of her skirt
and shouts, *Didn't you read my email?!*

I'm like, well yeah, sort of,
but I didn't see any—
and I let it trail off because, I don't know
what it was I didn't see. Eventually she
goes away and I make a concerted effort
to remember to check my email later.

One young man is struggling, he says his grandmother died.

He's got the fat salty poisonous tears and I just let him rip. I tell him we should make her a drawing and he does and I tell him the troll's story about the spaceship.

Okay, I say. I'm not comfortable looking people in the eye. But I look him right in the eye and I say, Okay. Tell me about your grandmother. He talks for five minutes, honestly she could be anyone's grandmother.

So I ask (because this is how the story goes)
Did you and your grandmother have a special place that you would go?

Without pause he says, *The roof!*
The roof?

Yeah we sat on the roof by the window it was really nice.
Did you drink tea on the roof.

No! We drank hot cocoa, and he said it like
the thought of drinking tea on the roof was
completely nuts.

Okay, so you're on the roof with Granny.

Gr-and-mother, he proclaims.

Yeah on the roof with your grandmother
and she's telling you a story about your—
wait mom's mom or dad's mom?

My mom's mom.

Oh yeah she is telling you a story about
your mom and drinking cocoa and it's a
really funny story and you know your mom
is going to be really mad and the story is so
great and you can't wait to hear how it ends
but your grandmother is tired and while she's
telling it she falls asleep and you want to hear
the end but she looks so peaceful so you sip
your cocoa and watch her.

Stillness.

Then a moth flies down. Only it really isn't a moth, but it's also definitely not a spaceship, but if it was anything it was more like a spaceship than a moth and then you start to realize it's kinda huge, and there's no window and no door, but something like a door opens up and there is a thing inside and it has no head, eyes or mouth, but you can feel it's looking at you and even though it doesn't have a mouth it speaks to you and do you know what it says?

What?

It says it's your Grandmother's turn to get on the ship.

No shit?

No shit, she's going on the ship and she's always going to be warm and she's never going to have sore legs or hands and she's going on a trip first to the moon then right through the sun and then she's going to Pluto — which is a planet by the way — and she'll eat candy for dinner and drink wine or water and she gets to see everything in the universe and do anything she wants, but it's her turn to get on the ship and it's not yours and you can't come on and you really shouldn't try and stop her and you realize it's a chance of a lifetime, and you want her to be happy but you also want to hear how the story about your mom ends and you know you're never going to hear the end of the story and you're never going to drink hot cocoa with your grandmother on the roof again. So what do you do?

He sighs. The light coming from his ears changed from purple to red to orange to yellow and he takes a big breath and says, *I know, I know it's my grandmother's turn to go on the ship, but I just don't want her to go.*

Doesn't really matter though, does it?

I know. If you got to go, then you just got to go. He looks up at me with puffy eyes and says, *You're pretty smart, but you're kind of a shitty art teacher.*

I am?

Yeah.

How so?

You never tell us what to do.

That's what a teacher does, they tell you what to do? I look at him a long time, the light is turning from yellow to green.

You want me to teach you something?

Yeah.
I point to the paper he's been scratching on.
    What do you call that?

It's a pencil. I already knew that.
    What do you do with a pencil?

I'm drawing (duh is implicit).
    What do you think drawing is?

He wobbles his pencil around, making marks
and scratches.

Like this.
    No not like this!
I put my hand on his hand to stop him.
    Drawing can mean lots of things, it could
mean pulling water from a well it could be
pulling a drawer. It could be doing this on the
paper, but what do you think drawing really is?

He pulls his hand across the paper.

This!

I put both my hands near his face and pull my palms to my eyes.

It's looking. It's really seeing.
(I'm gripping bits of light and pulling my hands to my eyes.) It is really seeing, it's drawing the light into my eyes.

He is stunned. *Drawing?*
Yeah drawing.
Oh shit.
Don't talk that way.
You did.
Who are they going to believe kid, you or me?

Drawing, he murmurs.
You know how to make yellow?

You can't make yellow it's a primary.
He mocks me.
    Unga Bunga I say and squeeze
tangerine orange and bright green
on a piece of paper, and I mix it into a
solid sandpoop.
I add water and drag my finger through it
and it lightens to banana yellow.

I mix magenta and orange and
make red.
I mix magenta and cyan and
make the deepest blue.

His eyeballs do not fall out onto the table.

    I don't teach you anything?

I don't think you are teaching me the things
you are supposed to be teaching me.

Do you feel better now?

Yellow light comes out of his ears. *I do.*
    Be nice for grandmother, she knows
everything you ever did and everything
you are ever going to do.

Oh shit, he says.
    Don't talk like that, you little turd.

I go to the staffroom and rummage in
the fridge for something to eat. I'm not
hungry I just like eating other peoples
food. I find a lamb kebab in a plastic
container and I take it for the troll,

I figure I owe him.

I'm not growing potatoes today
and I won't be butchering a pig
but I'm still going to want to eat
so I guess rather than feeling
so damn sorry for myself
I better get out of bed
and find a way to
keep the people
in this village
this earth
glad that
I am part
of this life
and some forgiveness
for the people who can not see
past wanting more (for less)
and just be glad I can
stand still and face
one more day
we all trudge
past the same
sunny meadows
we all want to lay
down in the grass
and later we will all
want to eat a potato
we all drink from wells
we did not dig

Scan

SIX

I DRIVE BACK TO THE CITY and pick up Jess
on the way. We stop for sushi. We eat fast
and we drive. She says she needs to pick up
cash from the bank and I want to print off
some images for reference.

Eight years ago I opened an art gallery and it
started like this:

Have an idea.
It's energy
It's free
Let it grow. Fester.
Don't sit, it seeps out
and will impregnate someone else.
Draw. Write. Shape. Sculpt.
Shove or let go.
Shove.
Find a space. Big. Bright and dirty.
If it's dirty and no one would set
foot inside, it's for you
if it's bright.

Pull down walls
the ragged ones in the basement
the fence outside
the matter between the homeless
and the owners
the walls suffocate communities
gravity, economics and science
pull down the walls that
keep people out and make it free
it will take time for the shock to
wear off. Hit 'em hard when they're dizzy

Clean up. Scrub. Paint.
there's thirteen drug needles in the parking lot.
That's your security deposit.
Dumpster after dumpster.
Hug. Kiss. Whisper.
It's yours as long as you pinch a fist.
Fight. Boy you'll paint with one hand
and ball the other.
Crazy people need love too.
Sometimes they get rough.
Be rough boy, be rough and gentle
don't get hurt
Keep the little ones safe
pretty girls and rich people and that
guy with no pants
and the gaping crowd

It's scary throwing out those needles.
Be scary boy. This old building
is coming down so you can rent it.
Keep it clean. Not too clean mind you.
Keep it safe.
Beautiful is on the inside.
Take a risk boy. Have me.
I'm yours.

• • •

It's Wednesday and we're not ready. The car rolls into the parkade by 4:30, Jess goes straight to the bank I run up fifteen flights of stairs tear off my teacher clothes put on a paint-stained shirt and jeans. We meet up on the way back to the gallery. If this is the part of the story you find hard to believe then I'm afraid there's really nothing I can do. I have an art gallery a block from my apartment. We tidy up the gallery. It's a mess every week because I use it as a paint studio evenings and weekends. Tonight it becomes a circus.

We walk in, 5 o'clock and it's covered in paint and sawdust and debris from the week's worth of building. It's a race against time because at 7 o'clock people start showing up for our event.

At 5:35 people start showing up for our event. Jeeze, we open at 7. Garbage, tables, put my stuff away power tools, paint, staples, screws, nails chunks of wood, clean the toilet, get rid of beer bottles, lids on things, records away, people show up, try and be nice, shit out everywhere, people setting up, try and be nice, we set the place up, it's hot already, turn on the fan, there are people everywhere, Jess smiles, boots up and the spotlights—

Good evening everyone, welcome to the Rumble House. In the center of the room our hostess stands on something like a table, maybe it's a stage, and she spins a wheel and it lands on a book and she opens it and reads from it.

She reads from
Alexander Eliot's Site and Insight, Page 4—

It is better to receive than to give — up to a point. After that point the reverse is equally true. In fact there comes a time when if a man is not a source he is a sewer. The true artist has disciplined and filled and freed himself for giving. He is a bottomless cup that keeps welling full and running over.

Then she spins the wheel again. It lands
on a book of magic and she splits the
book open and yells, *Baba Yaga!*

She spins the wheel a third time and it
lands on an empty space from the first
book so we follow the trajectory of the
arrow across the room and it lands on a
stack of books. We pull Orpheus from
the top of the stack and our hostess, Jess,
announces the themes of the night are:
If you are not a source you are a sewer,
the Baba Yaga, and Orpheus chasing his
love into hell.

I walk up to the plank of wood I'd
meant to work on, it feels all wrong, I
push it aside and rummage through my
supports, I find a frame stretched with
denim instead of canvas, it's bigger than
I wanted, it was a long day and I was
hoping to sit down tonight but I pull out
my easel and mount the frame and
I step back looking and waiting
for the image to appear.

Nothing

Baba Yaga
Nothing

A man is a source
Nothing

Black Orpheus, I do get a bit of a pang, but no one wants the devil in their kitchen, if they do they aren't going to help me make rent tonight.

Devil, Orpheus, the hero, Black, no blue, Baba, Moth, Minotaur, Baba, moth, a broken heart—

Shit, Nothing.

People are walking up and saying hello and they are happy to see me and they want to know about my day and they need gesso and they want a canvas and they wonder if I'd like a cookie, and I'm screaming on the inside and smiling on the outside. I look away and I look at them and I look at the canvas and I see this one thread.

It's moving like a teeny tiny worm. It's unrolling and the whole canvas (sorry denim) opens up from the center and my friend the troll pokes his eye through and I poke him in the eye with the end of my brush.

I step back and I reach into my backpack and shove the stolen container of lamb into the canvas. He pokes his tongue through, blows a wet raspberry at me and disappears.

Through the hole climbs out a very faint Jezebel. She winks at me and sits, she's wearing a potato sack, but she is wearing it well, she crawls out of the rip in the canvas and spreads her legs—

Woman. Please. She crosses her legs and builds a fire, she pulls a pot out of nowhere and starts cooking a fat leg of a lamb.

Eye-of-newt, a few other things. I'm not sure if anyone wants the Baba Yaga in their living room but it's too late now and I start to trace out her shoulders and elbows with my brush, I start with the lightest spots slicing into the dark indigo night with white paint strokes showing the world where her long fingers and short arms should be.

She sits very still so I can trace her, but she doesn't like when I split my attention, so when someone speaks to me she moves just a little while I'm looking away.

It goes on like this for a while and then she's emerged, the rest is a matter of putting on a play to make it look like I am working harder than I am. I'll need to make rent in the auction, and people want to know I've earned my way.

There's a disturbance outside, then the toilet gets clogged, there are two large spills, a lost wallet and a few other things.

By 9 pm we drag all the tables out the front door switch off the fluorescents, turn on the spot lights and we auction off 30 or 40 paintings.

By 11 the crowd thins and Jess sings us some Billie Holiday and I lie and say if they don't get out I'm going to padlock them in until morning.

Half the money of each of the paintings, all of hers and all of mine add up to exactly one fifth of the month's rent. Which is lucky because this particular June happens to have five Wednesdays before July.

We lock up and walk home. My minotaur friend waves at me from inside the window, posing as though he's going to tip over a lamp.

Scan

SEVEN

T HE NEXT DAY AT SCHOOL is murky soup. I
don't think I hurt anyone and the paintings
in my classroom are as good as the paintings at
my art gallery, so people mostly leave me alone.
When teachers ask me for paper to use in the
other classrooms, I start telling them all about
paper. Did you know almost all paper has one
way you can rip a straight line, I say and I rip a
perfectly straight line one way, and then I show
them that with the exact same effort if I try
and rip the paper the other way it goes all over
the place and rips like the peaks of the Rocky
Mountains. This paper will start to degrade
in months, see it's starting to fade, this other
paper will last a thousand years, and if a lesson
on paper doesn't drive the other teachers away,
I show them where I keep the large sheets of
paper, I only order super large sheets, and then I
point them to the paper cutter.

This way I never have to worry about my
budget.

If the paper lesson didn't drive them away having to size their own paper does.

. . .

A student walks in and asks for a piece of paper, I ask what for? She says she is making a social project, so I give her the thousand-year paper, she sits at the lunch table outside my door with a pile of clippings and pulls the cap off her glue stick.

You know how to use that thing?

This? She says holding out the glue stick

Yeah, anyone ever show you how to use that?

She smears glue on the paper and fwaps it down.

Nice, good technique.

Flat. Kind of perfect.

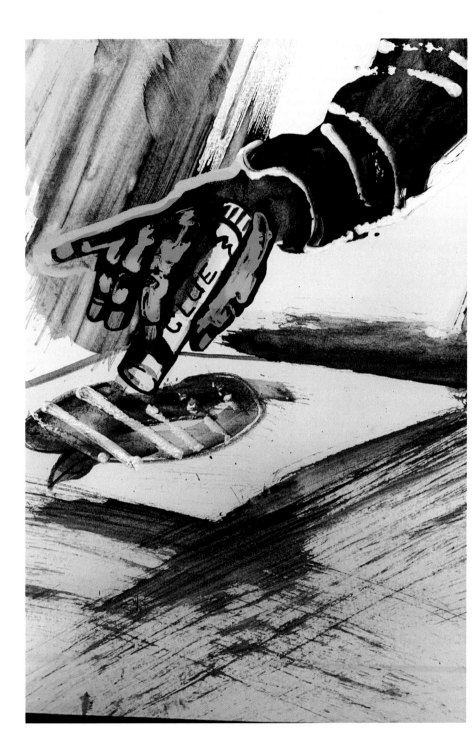

When is your project due?
Monday.
Won't the paper curl and dry and peel
off by Monday?

Yeah?! Right?? she says, like this is a thing
everyone knows but no one ever talks about.

Is it just a stupid product? Why do they
even sell this junk?

She is actually agog.

If you apply the glue to the surface
of the paper and pat it down on the
other paper, it stays and looks flat, but by
tomorrow it peels off when it's dry. The
secret is to apply glue to both the surface of
the thing you are gluing and the thing you
are gluing on. So the glue is sticking to glue,
not glue sticking to paper. I have a lesson on
sharpening a pencil too when you are ready.

How do I sharpen a pencil?

You are not ready, and I walk back to
my room. It only takes two giant steps.

· · ·

In the staff room. I know I said I never
go but I sit in the middle of an awkward
conversation. One of the new teachers is
struggling, she is trying to explain how
hard it is to meet new people once you start
teaching.

It's a trap, you were surrounded by single
young people all through university, but you
dump your partner so you can survive those
first two years of teaching and then you find
yourself surrounded by old married people,
and you don't get out much because of all
the marking.

Yeah, says everyone.
        Teaching in a high school, by the end of
the year you are already starting to see the
students at the bar.

Yeah! everyone says.

They each take a turn to tell a funny story
about leaving the bar or pub because their
students walked in.

It's worse for you guys because you
live in a small town.

Yeah!
I was thinking it should be kind of
an unspoken rule that the union reps
should be single, then all the single
people would be fighting over who gets to
go to the union meetings.

Yeah! They all say.

If I knew they were all so agreeable,
I'd probably spend more time
in the staff room.

Sometimes I feel like we are all living out
plots for TV sitcoms. The new teacher
says, *I don't feel like I need to be in a
relationship to justify—*

I say, It doesn't matter, it's okay to be
independent, but we're built in halves.

I pull a sheet of paper
off the shelf behind me
and reach for her pen.

We are built in halves, and I draw a half circle, And you have to be a whole half, and you really shouldn't be more than a whole half, that's no good either.

But we are built in halves, and there are almost eight billion people in the world and, you know there is a tallest person in the world and a shortest person in the world. I'm the heaviest person in this room and you are probably the lightest, weight and height are easier to measure than volume—

I realize I owe the troll more lamb.

It's not easy to measure volume, but there is a tallest person in the world and a shortest person in the world.

Yeah, I guess, she says.
So we are built in halves and you have to be a whole half, but consider out of eight billion people there is one worst match for you and one best match for you and when you find this person you will be whole—

And that whole half makes a perfect match and you become one whole circle and now you can really move.

What if I don't meet him?
Oh, no, there is no promise you will meet him. You just have to be ready. What are you doing so this person can find you?

I watch a lot of TV— (she giggles)
I don't know how he will find you in your living room. The odds are kind of against him just dropping by your house. It could happen.

Sometimes you are thinking you are getting through to people. Little signs of light in the eye, recognition in the face.

Just now I'm thinking of calling the school nurse. Because this young lady's face has gone quite pale and I think she might be in shock.

So, he's real, he's out there, but he might be in Mumbai?

Well if he is your one perfect match and if he was born in Mumbai, I would think something in him is pulling him here or something in you would be pulling you away. Right? That's part of what makes him the perfect match.

That seems a little too simple.
    I don't know. I kind of dreamed up Jess. I often wonder if she's real.

The minotaur pops his head out of the washroom and waves at me.

    Do you know what he looks like?

No, no that doesn't matter.
    Sure it does, how else will you find him?

Uh, no as long as he's—
    Not bald?

Oh, yeah I think I would like if he's not bald.

The tall girl blurts out *Bald guys are hot!*
    Exactly, I say, but no short guys.

Exactly.

Another lady at the table says, *I love short,
bald guys.*
Exactly, I say.

The point is we're not all beautiful but we're all
beautiful to someone.

Oh, you are right he's not tall he's average, says
the new teacher.
I start to draw him. What kind of hair?

Oh, I don't care, she shrugs.
Man bun?

Oh yes I think man bun.
Beard?

Yes.
Better without the beard, you can ask
him to grow one but you wouldn't want to
find you don't like his face if he shaves it off.
We sit and I draw her other half and in about
twenty minutes he starts looking real. I hand
her the paper and she folds it.

You put that in your wallet.

And what do I do with it, run up to some guy in the mall and show him I drew his picture.
I can think of worse things.

She folds it carefully and loads it into a pink wallet behind her credit cards.

You won't find him until you are ready to find him.

What if I find him and he's married?
Look, I say reassuringly, this is my dream, I'll see that you find your prince before I wake up.

This can't be your dream because I know I'm real.
Of course you'd say that.
I get in the car and drive away leaving my moose-headed friend chasing me. He almost catches up at the red light but before I get to the highway I blow right through it and drive home to Jess.

On Thursday nights we run a nude figure
drawing class at the gallery. It's warm and
comfortable, but not nearly as racy as it
sounds. As many people come as it takes to
pay the model. Our status is breaking even.
We sit we draw we leave the desks out and
we go home. I've helped so many people
today and I know I've earned a good sleep.

Scan

EIGHT

WE GO HOME, drink coffee on the balcony and listen to a record on our outdoor phonograph. We brush our teeth, Jess washes off her face, and we fall asleep easy. It's always easy when I've had a giving day and today I gave it my all.

The problem with falling asleep early is I always wake up. I dress, walk out into the warm wind and make my way down to the river. I go over the bridge, down the steps by the war memorial with a chunk of lamb from the fridge. I am in great debt to my troll.

We're made of ancient suns
fuelled by the fire of sol
we're meant to burn
Burn Mother Burn

Under the bridge. Baba Yaga.
Not my Jess' Baba Yaga. This one is real.
She's stewing up a giant pot.
It's not at all like the pot I imagined.

She's crushing up magpie and duck with her mortar, no eye of newt. She doesn't speak, she just glares, pours the bird purée into the pot. I can see the green foot of my troll floating in the soup. I throw my hucking leg of lamb in the pot and walk away.

· · ·

It's a foggy soup the rest of the night and the rest of the day. I'm totally aware I'm alive for a moment getting ready for work. I know I shouldn't, but I stick a Q-tip in my ear. You're not supposed to stick it in your ear, but it feels so good. I gently roll it in my deaf ear and I try not to fall asleep it feels so good.

Fridays are more forgiving. People start to check out at lunch time. They check out Friday at lunch, and they start stressing and checking back in some time around noon on Sunday.

If you live 70 years, you've got 50 years of Sunday to Friday, and only 20 years of Friday to Sunday. Not counting getting sick or bad news on the weekend, that's a pretty unfavorable split.

There's pizza in the cafeteria at lunch and I make it through the edgy teenagers without saying anything stupid or mean. My inside voice is downright horrible.

My outside voice is mostly okay. I haven't seen my minotaur today. I hope he wasn't in the soup too. I stop by the counselor's office, and she winks because she knows I'm fuggin nuts and I think she finds it's amazing I can negotiate my way through the day posing as a teacher.

I might have a coffee before I drive home, do you want one?

No, Jeeze if I drink coffee this late in the day I'll be up all night.
Really? I drink coffee because it helps me sleep.

She roars with laughter, *Of course you do!*
She has read a lot of text books about people like me. But I think she earnestly likes me, she's one of the reasons I can negotiate my way.

I get in the car
          still no sign of my minotaur.

Flow over
Be a river son
The mountains are
Tall and you can flow
All year, all day, all night
Without fear of running dry
Be a river son and overflow
With love for your brothers
and sisters and hope and love
There's no bank for it
There's no safe
Be unsafe
Flow across
The whole world

Splash the cities with
Your indiscriminate love
Splash the people and
Their cars and wash
their feet in your wake
flush the sewers
Be unstoppable
Be fearless
Be the river true

Scan

NINE

Mᴜᴄʜ ᴡɪʟᴅᴇʀ than my minotaur or the
troll under the bridge is my seven year old.
I pick him up from his mother's house.
She is a nice lady, very linear. There is a list of
things I am to remember before I return our
child Sunday around noon.

He's out the door without shoes, we jam his
bike into the hatch of my little car, I grab shoes
and a hat but I do forget the list of things I was
supposed to remember.

We play a game in the car. It's a game we
invented for his least imaginative teacher.
He asks me a question that could be an authentic
classroom question and I answer the most
outlandish answer I can imagine.
It's harder than it sounds—

What is the distance around the Earth?
   Oh, Oh, I know, Meatballs!

It's harder than it seems because one is tempted
to answer a correct answer and the outlandish

ones are only funny if they are a certain distance off the mark. We play this game and drive on to pick up Jess.

It's sunny and warm and we go get pizza and buy some records, and ride our bikes over the bridges until the late evening sun goes down.

I get him home before dark. God knows what demons run amok in his little head. But I see his hands moving and his lips moving, having conversations with them. He doesn't like when I ask him about it.

He has teddy bears but he hides them meticulously until he thinks we are asleep and then lines them up at the edge of the bed. One night last year (no, he wasn't around that night) Jess and I walked home from the gallery and a rather nonchalant police officer informed us that we could go home but to use the back door, and to please not step on the tarpaulin. We went inside and put on a movie. I was curious and so I put my phone camera over the edge of the balcony and I time-lapse videoed the ground from the fifteenth floor. When I played back the video I watched them remove the tarp, pick up several parts of a body and reassemble the fella

from the 19th floor onto a gurney. I was really
sorry I filmed that.
That was a private moment for him.
And I was deeply sorry.

I carried a lot of guilt about this until this very
night. In the middle of the night my son gets out
of bed and says, *The neighbor is falling Dad.*
What ?

He's falling. And he's happy.
What?

Don't worry about it, he said, and he went back
to bed. I could hear him murmur, *Man you don't
get anything.*
Go pee! I yell.

I don't have to! he yells back.
Go Pee!

Gawd! And he does and we all go to sleep.

We get letters from school warning to check
the kids for lice. I'm looking for signs of antlers.
Tonight though, I sleep. I don't even dream.

It's strange for me to wake up and see him
standing there looking at me. He seems
disappointed I'm not up yet. I'm unused to
having people see me sleeping. Ever. Somehow
this kid is an even more tightly bound bundle of
energy than me.

Dad do you know what people are thinking?
Sometimes. Do you?

He doesn't answer, but then I think I hear him
say I said, *no I don't.* And I think yeah you do
and he says emphatically, *No I don't!*

Scan

TEN

WE RUMBLE OVER and turn the Saturday cartoons on. He likes (mostly) the same shows I watched when I was a kid. He also likes the ones made in Japan, they overdub and the lips never match up and there is always one puffy character that can't speak but who makes an unbearable screeching noise. Kids like this noise. At some point we all put the couch pillows on the floor and pretend the living room carpet is lava. We all make the same noise for machine guns and the same broom broom sound for a car, but for some reason children love the screeching unintelligible yelp of the puffy character.

It is the opposite of baroque or broccoli— as they outgrow the screechy puffy character, they start to crave that high E rip off of Louis Armstrong's hot trumpet. We pack drawing pads and ride bikes to the zoo, or the city art gallery. Wherever we go, in case we want to sit we bring art supplies. I realize I'm pretty happy almost all of the time.

I have a speaker strapped to my bike and I
ride around blasting music. People either
really hate it, or they really love it and I
am happy to facilitate both of those needs.
Jess overcompensates pretending she is
comfortable — I have to be careful I don't
take her for granted. What is a lout like me
supposed to do with a lady this beautiful, so
willing to try out anything I can think of. Not
taking advantage is a full time job. I'm not sure
what she's thinking most of the time.

At least I'm careful about the music I choose,
everyone loves Johnny Cash, Bowie, and
Bob Dylan, and if they don't they probably
deserve whatever discomfort I've caused them.

God damn psychopaths.

At night I put my son into bed and we listen
to records until he falls asleep. In the morning
he goes home to his mother and the week
starts again.

There's a moment on Sunday afternoon when
I can do anything I want, as long as anything
I want means building frames and putting
right the things that have been broken or are
wearing out in the gallery.

Jess buys us a bottle of wine and we plug away
at setting the stage for the coming Wednesday.
If things stay steady or pick up a little I won't
have to pull an all nighter to make and sell a
painting to my good friend and benefactor.

I make about four frames. I'll stretch them
later. Everyone else I know is sweating this
afternoon away, dreading Monday, but I've
found a space where every day is a little good
and every day is just a bit evil, and so I float,
neutral buoyancy never waiting for anything.

My nemesis knocks loudly on the door, walks
into the space to see my painting. He can
only make things with his projector, or on
see-through mylar and I find he drops by to
check up on my realism. Sometimes I think he
draws faint grid lines on his large canvases to
imply he drew his work on his own, though the
lines on the canvas and lines on his reference

photo don't line up. Disingenuous evidence
he used a grid to form such a highly realistic
reproduction? I don't care if he uses a projector.
I don't see how it's any better or worse than
tracing ghosts on my own canvas.

Where's your big pink Lady?
    Sold it.
*Oh you sold that one, don't you think you should
keep a few for the archives?*
    No. Not really.
What did it go for if you don't mind me asking?

    LISTEN MOTHER FUGGER FUGG OFF
I KNOW YOU SELL FOR MORE THAN I
DO BUT AT LEAST I CAN DRAW MY OWN
FUGGING DRAWINGS WITHOUT ANY
HELP FROM A MACHINE YOU ONE TRICK
LEONARDO DAVINCI LIGHT BULB TRACER
FUGGING PONY.

    It sold for more than a table and less than a
couch.
You know you don't charge enough.
    Right, well they aren't very hard to make
and I find I'd be painting if they didn't sell
anyway so it's for the best to move them out of
the way.

Yeah well you make it hard on everyone else, not everyone has a second cushy job to fall back on.

CUSHY ?!? I SPEND HALF AN HOUR A DAY TALKING TO A MAGIC UNICORN MAN DRESSED LIKE A GOAT TO KEEP MYSELF FROM DRIVING INTO THE MOUNTAINS AND TYING MY SELF TO A TREE COVERED IN PEANUT BUTTER HOPING TO ATTRACT A GRIZZLY IN HEAT YOU SPOILED TRUST-FUND MAMMA'S BABY

How's the new studio?
It's okay I could always use a larger space.
Right. What are you working on now?
A few commissions.
Nice. Can I offer you a drink?
No, I'm off to the Flim Flam opening,
you should go.
I would, but my immediate attention is required right here.

He leaves and I recalculate my pricing index. I make about three hundred dollars an hour for my actual painting time, but I don't keep any of the money and I only make that much because people want to keep this place alive. I'm not sure how my nemesis pays the bills, maybe a rich uncle. Most of the working artists I know complain about having to make a living off their sales but most of them don't pay taxes and couldn't lease their vehicles if they didn't have someone in their lives supporting them.

Not that I'm complaining.

I spit at the door as he leaves. He's shaken my confidence enough that he shouldn't need to feed again for a while and the other people at that opening should be better off.

In contrast, a tiny white spider crawls over my hand and then scoots across the table. It draws a tiny white line right off the edge and up to the bookshelf, it burrows in a book gifted to me from one of my former art school instructors.

Last Christmas this instructor called me in the middle of dinner and dropped off a book of his work as a gift. Turns out he's one of the most genuine people I've ever met. For years I thought I didn't like him.

We take from our teachers, absorb their knowledge, and then we eat them.

I considered telling him how wrong I had
been about him when he gave me the book. I
considered turning down the gift. Either way it
meant I'd have to admit I didn't like him.
It was a pleasure to discover I was wrong. And
now I wonder, in a decade or few, will I discover
my nemesis is more wonderful than I imagine?
I pull several tables together and turn on the
fake fireplace, Jess flips records and we start
mind mapping some art lesson plans.

WHY DO WE MAKE ART?

1) An impulse to modify. You just can't avoid this, but if you try, you tend to get destructive. Why do people dye their hair or grow gardens in their yard? We make art because we have a compulsion to modify.

2) An urge to communicate. One never can. Our brains are shielded from each other by thick skulls. I often wonder if animals think more as groups, most animals, but not humans, and not dogs, rather dogs attach to humans and humans seem to have gone dormant within themselves. But we make art, sing songs, write poetry, dance, make potpourri and so on, and so we to try and make a human connection.

3) To share big ideas. Any time you try and work out a really big idea, the idea expands faster than words can manage, you get out a pen to write notes, but as the idea grows you have to draw. Really big ideas you have to draw, so one of the reasons we draw is to take on the really big ideas.

4) In search of quality. This is the domain of the realists, does a magpie look like a magpie, are the arms too short for her majesty's body? This is the canon of the photo copier. Like those damn photos of women swimming in red dresses underwater—you couldn't even pretend you were drawing from life.

5) To establish permanence. If not through art, then at least through purchasing property or putting your name on things, we see permanence. In the worst case scenario, parenting. We want to live forever, like vampires, so we enroll our kids in the things we dreamed of and failed. That said my kids seem to love to paint, and so my parenting, though selfish, maybe isn't all bad.

So, asks Jessica, *what makes good art?*

Answers in art come in fives and I expected it would line up with our five reasons for making art. But they don't, it feels like it should be five.

We sit down and eventually we realize it starts with a search for quality. Methodically it grows from there.

———————

MASTERY: Formal surface composition.
Focus. Unity. Balance. Movement.
Rhythm. Contrast. Pattern. Proportion.
Line. Color. Shape. Form. Value. Space.
Texture. Contour lines. Symmetry.
Foreshortening. Terminology. Iconography.
Assemblage. Paint Strokes. Quality of Line.
Chroma. Conceptual Art. Chiaroscuro.

All the things we look at in art class
(technique)
does your apple look like an apple?

———————

INVESTMENT: Time spent. Is it big?
Did it take a long time to do?
Is there a lot of it? Did you put your ten
thousand hours into making it?
This is exactly how Picasso could
draw a bull in seconds.

TRUTHFULNESS:
My little brother could do that!
The absence of that feeling you are being
hustled. Vincent Van Gogh versus
Barnett Newman.

REACH: Does it communicate?
Does something come across? The Sender
Receiver Model. Does the viewer get
anything from it?

SOUL: *Je ne sais quoi.* Jazz.
That magic feeling in your tummy.
That thing your art school instructors
kept to themselves.

Scan

———————————

ELEVEN

I'M EXHAUSTED, we pack up and go home.

I can't sleep, wait a second I do sleep, no I'm
awake, it's the middle of the night, it's only the
start of the week, I know better than to check
my phone but I do and just at that moment one
of the lost boys texts me and asks if he's okay
to come to figure drawing. Of course. He's low,
one of his friends died. This happens a lot, I
chat with him and I think I make a difference
and then I fall asleep and then he and I and the
minotaur are in the interesting room.

The clever monkey is explaining we are built in
halves.

I interrupt: I say to the lost boy—
    What if your friend was in that place you
go before you are born and the director told him
he was too early to go back, he would be either
too early or too late to find his other half. Your
friend was longing to breathe, he says, could
I just go back for a little while? The fun part, I
won't floss, could I go down for the first bit and

come back here so it all lines up … and then and then—

…and then I'm awake.

I put on a loose sweater, fresh jeans and I'm out the front door again. There is a chill, I wish I took a jacket on my way out the door, the wind is heavy and the sky is black and the sticks and loose bits of garbage do back flips down the street. I go around my path not wanting to go under the bridge.

But sitting with one foot in the river is my troll.

Whoa, I thought the Baba Yaga got you.

She did not.
Oh man what happened?

She ate my foot.
Yeah, That's a grind my friend.

It's no bother, I've got another one.
He holds up his stump with the better part of a tree strapped to it.

I'll find something more permanent when I'm done feeling bloody sorry for myself. It's a shame about your moose-headed friend though.

I don't ask.

Do you— he trails off. *Can I ask, do you ever think of anyone but yourself?*
    No, I say. Its my curse and my gift.

How so?
    Well I'm pretty vain and I'm wrapped up in my own ego, but on the bright side, I'm not walking around telling everyone what they have to think and say.

Good show. I read somewhere if anyone ever tells you what you're thinking you should eat them before they drive you fuggin' nuts.
    Uh, yeah I suppose.

I tell the troll about my nemesis, and the art planning and the teachers at my school and about my boy and about my other boy who isn't really part of this story and I thank him so much and we talk about lives and our futures and about how much his foot hurts and how he thinks he can kind of feel it rotting in the Baba Yaga's tummy.

We talk about losing things and gaining things and we talk about our homes and dreams.

I admit I'm a little bitter.

That I want the world to love me, but it seems like the world hates me.

He laughs. *You ungrateful ponce. I am a one-foot troll with no bridge.*

Ha ha, you are, and I spit at him and to add insult to injury the wind lifts it up and the spit flies up and hits him in the face.

I'll kill you for that, he says,
but he just wipes it off and licks his hand.

        You really are a gross mother fugger,
    I say.

Ha ha I am, he says, puts his thumb to
his index finger and flicks me the fugg a
hundred yards away.

Ringing in my ears, Duke Ellington says,
Let the world catch up with you.

I hope the one-eyed witch giantess is
waiting for me this time.

I hope she is ready.

Scan

ABOUT RICH THÉROUX

Besides being a caveman, Rich is a genius talent at painting and drawing. His art hangs here and there in prominent homes and galleries but he prefers not to boast about it. Rich is founder of Calgary's Rumble House gallery and happens to also teach junior high school art. He is the author and illustrator of *Stop Making Art and Die*, and the co-author of the poetry book, *A Wake in the Undertow*, along with his partner Jess Szabo. Intriguingly, he calls himself a tomato can. He and his gang exist/co-exist in Calgary, Alberta, Canada.